DATE DUE

DEMCO 38-297

The Princess
And
The Pea

The Princess
And
The Pea

Adapted from Hans Christian Andersen

and illustrated by *Janet Stevens*

Holiday House / New York

For Lindsey, with love

Copyright © 1982 by Janet Stevens
All rights reserved
Printed in the United States of America

Library of Congress Cataloging in Publication Data

Stevens, Janet.
The princess and the pea.

Adaptation of: Prindsessen paa âerten / by H. C.
Andersen.
Summary: A young girl feels a pea through twenty
mattresses and twenty featherbeds and proves that she
is a real princess.
[1. Fairy tales] I. Andersen, H. C. (Hans Christian),
1805-1875. Prindsessen paa âerten. II. Title.
PZ8.S614Pr   [E]   81-13395   AACR2
ISBN 0-8234-0442-0   ISBN 0-8234-0753-5 (pbk.)

There was once a prince who wanted to marry a princess.

According to his mother, the queen, she had to be a *real* princess, very much like herself.

So they traveled all over the world to find one.

They traveled to the east. "A *real* princess can play soft music on three instruments at once," said the queen. "This princess is too noisy."

They traveled to the west. "A *real* princess can skip across the lawn without bending the grass," said the queen. "This princess is too clumsy."

They traveled to the north. "A *real* princess can take small, dainty bites and never ask for seconds," said the queen. "This princess is too greedy."

They traveled to the south. "A *real* princess can dance with the grace of a swan on the head of a pin," said the queen. "This princess can't *possibly* be real."

"They just don't make princesses like they used to," said the queen. So at last the prince and his mother returned home. The prince was sad that they were unable to find a *real* princess. The queen was mad and disgusted.

One evening, there was a terrible thunderstorm. Rain poured down, and a great wind whistled through the town. When the storm was at its worst, there was a knock at the palace door. The old king went to open it.

Standing there was a princess. She was soaked, and water spilled out of her shoes and sleeves.

"I am a *real* princess," she said.

"You are?" asked the king. "Then you must meet the queen!"

When the king introduced them, the queen started to laugh.
"How can you be a *real* princess when you look like that?" she
asked.

"But I *am*," said the visitor.

"Well, my dear, it's very late. Stay for the night, and we can
discuss it in the morning," said the queen.

The queen had a plan. She hurried to a guest room and stripped the mattress from the bed. She laid a single pea on the bedstead.

Then she took twenty mattresses and piled them on top of the pea. She piled twenty feather beds on top of the mattresses. Now the bed was ready for the princess.

"This is where you are to sleep tonight," said the queen.

The princess was very tired. "I'm sure I'll sleep well on so many mattresses and beds," she said.

She climbed slowly up to the top and lay down.

"Good night," said the queen. "I do hope you sleep well."

The princess settled down into the bed. She rolled to the right, and she rolled to the left. She lay on her stomach, and she lay on her back. No matter how hard she tried, she could not find a comfortable position on such a rocky bed.

In the morning, the queen asked, "Did you sleep well?"
"No!" said the princess. "I tossed and turned all night. My
body is covered with bruises this morning!"

The queen gasped. "You didn't sleep? You must have felt the pea! Then you *are* a *real* princess. Only a *real* princess would have such delicate skin she could feel a pea through twenty mattresses and twenty feather beds."

So the prince married the princess. The entire kingdom was
invited to the wedding.

Even the queen was satisfied. She was so pleased to find a *real* princess, she put the famous pea in a museum where it can still be seen if no one has stolen it.